I Like Elephants

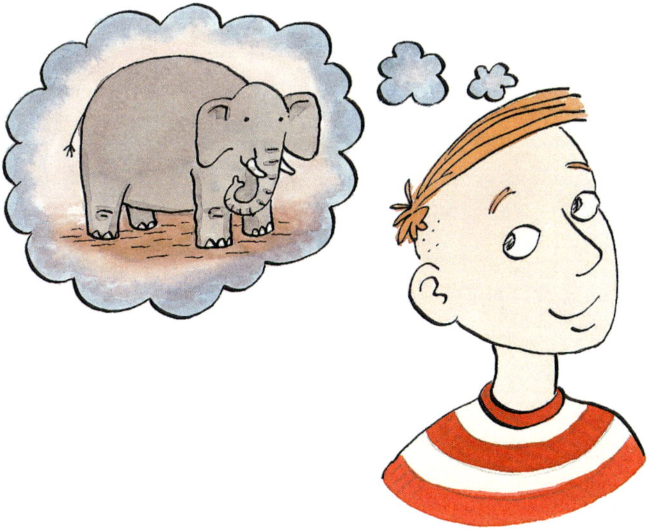

Illustrated by Trevor Pye

Rigby

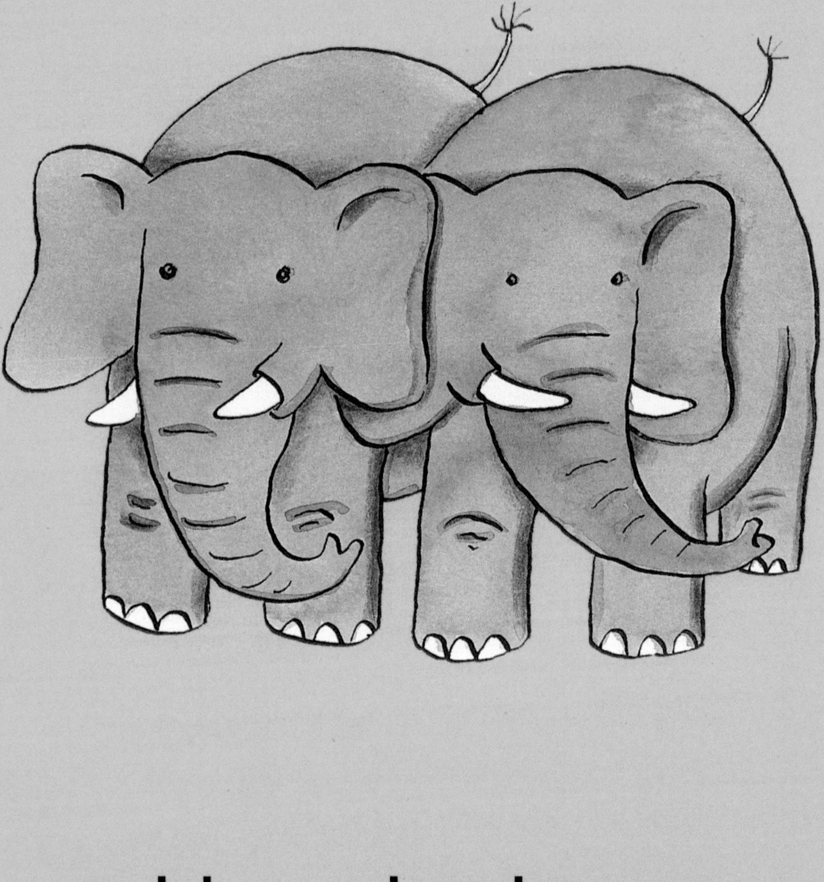

I like elephants.

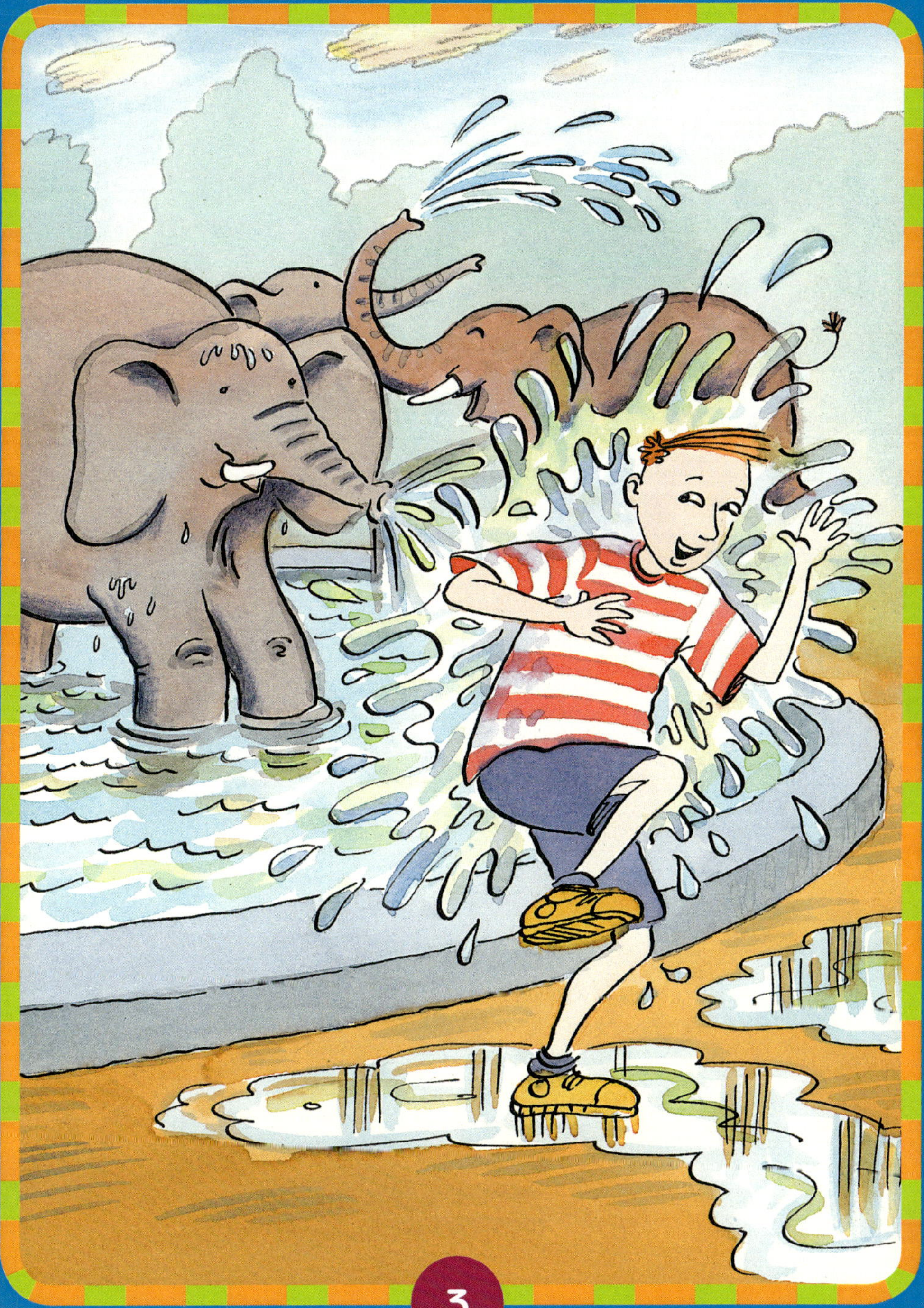

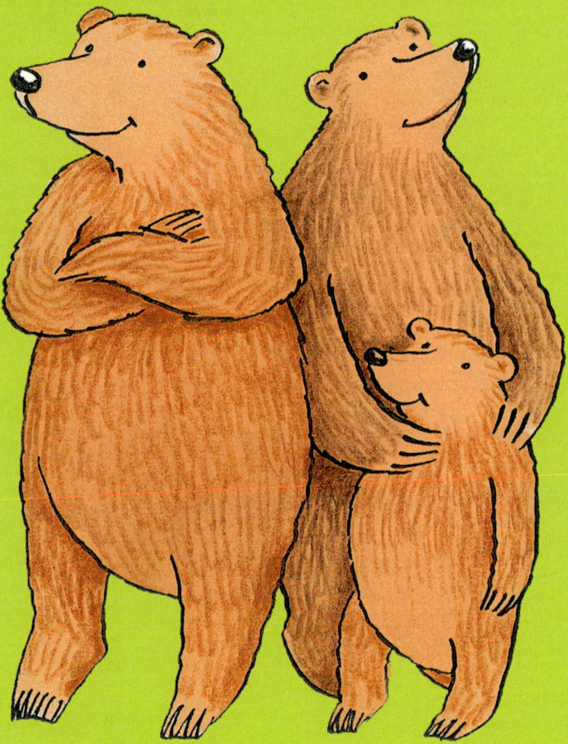

I like bears.

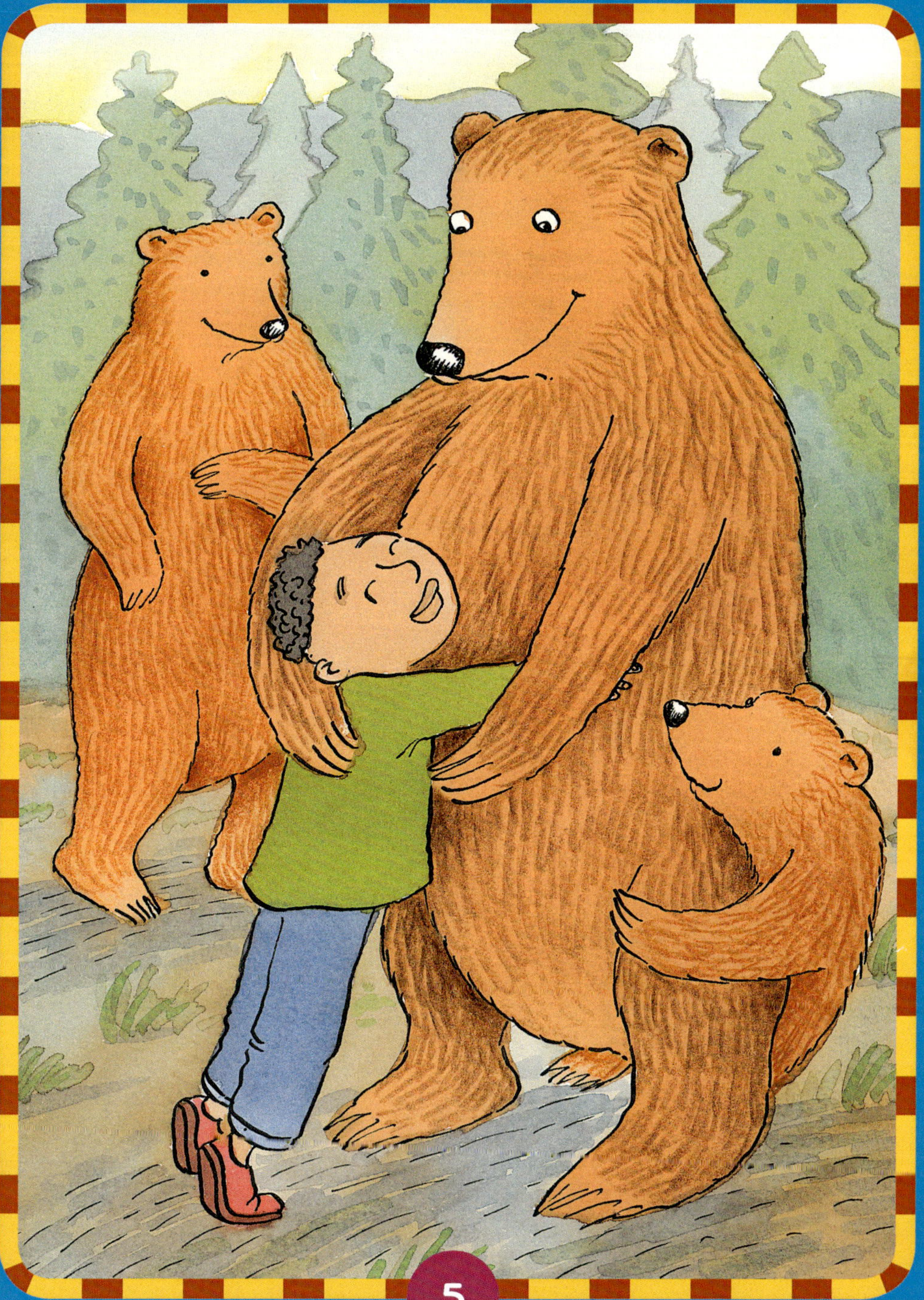

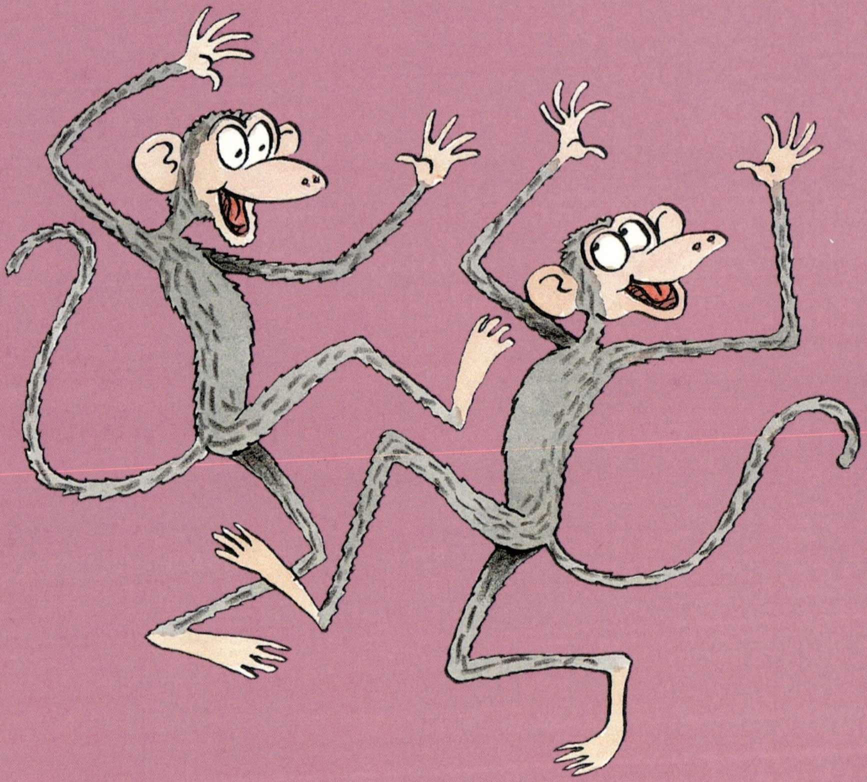

I like monkeys.

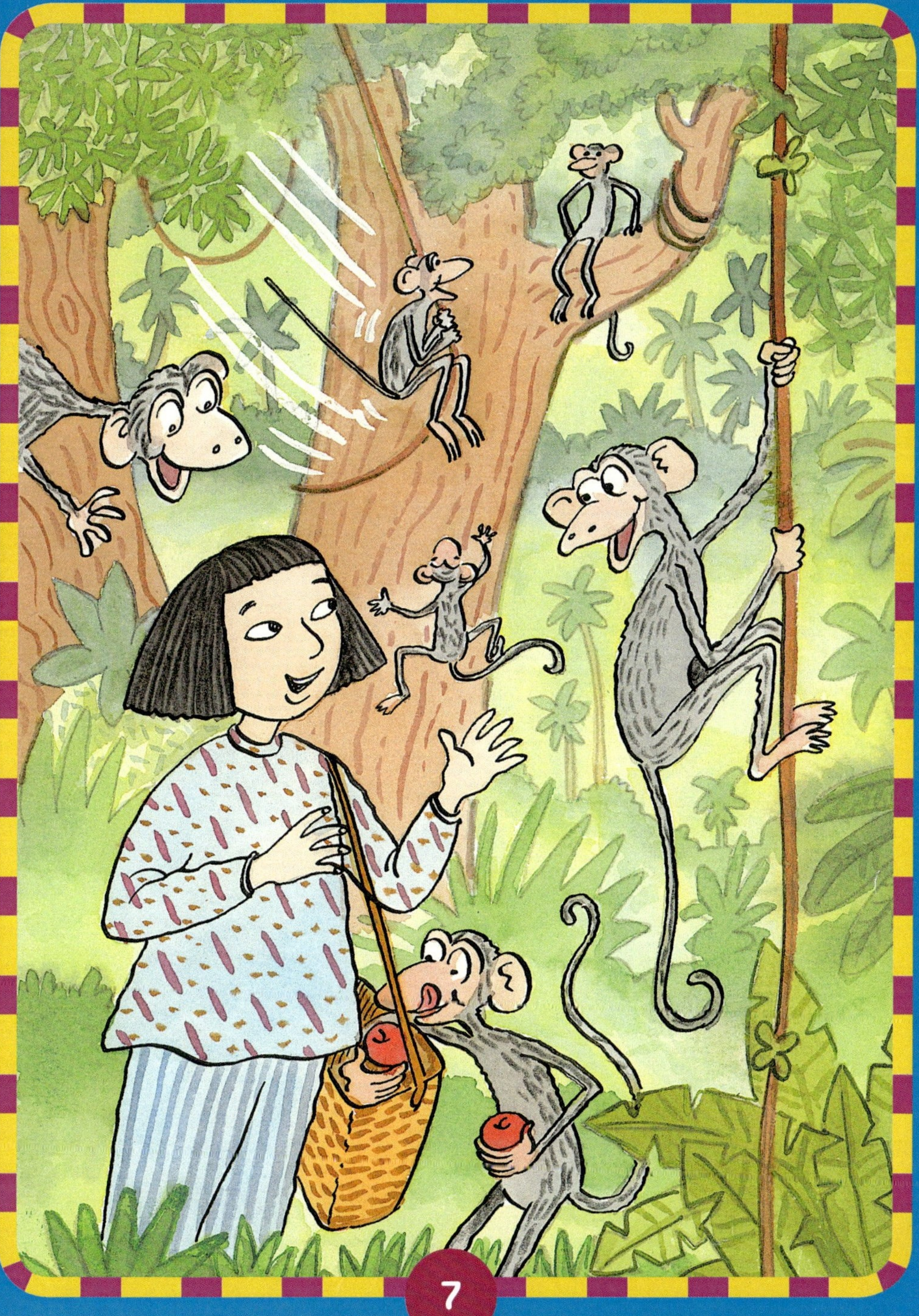

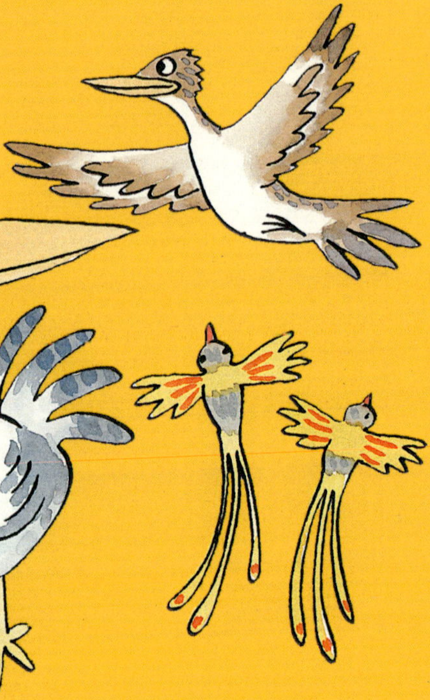

I like birds.

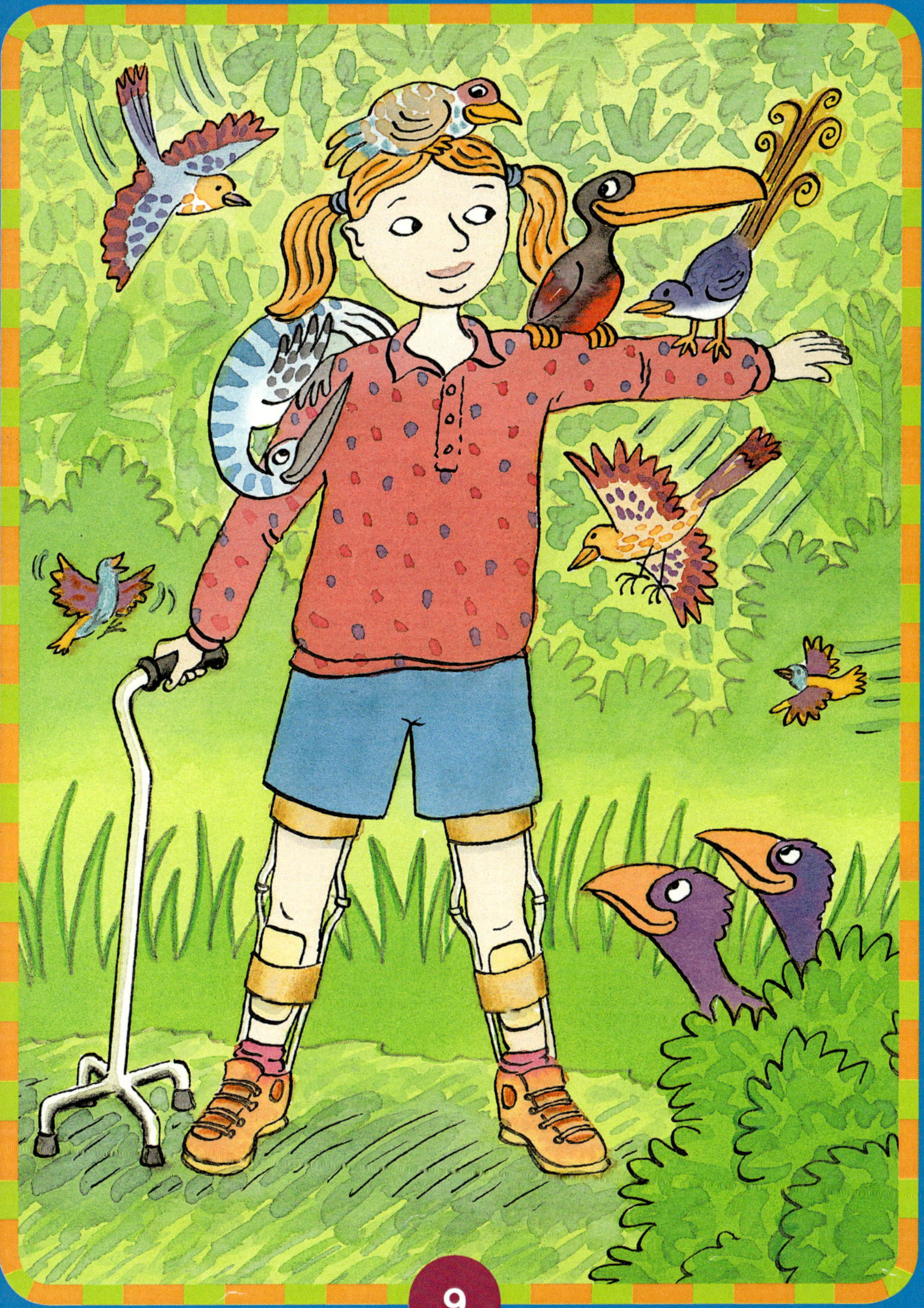

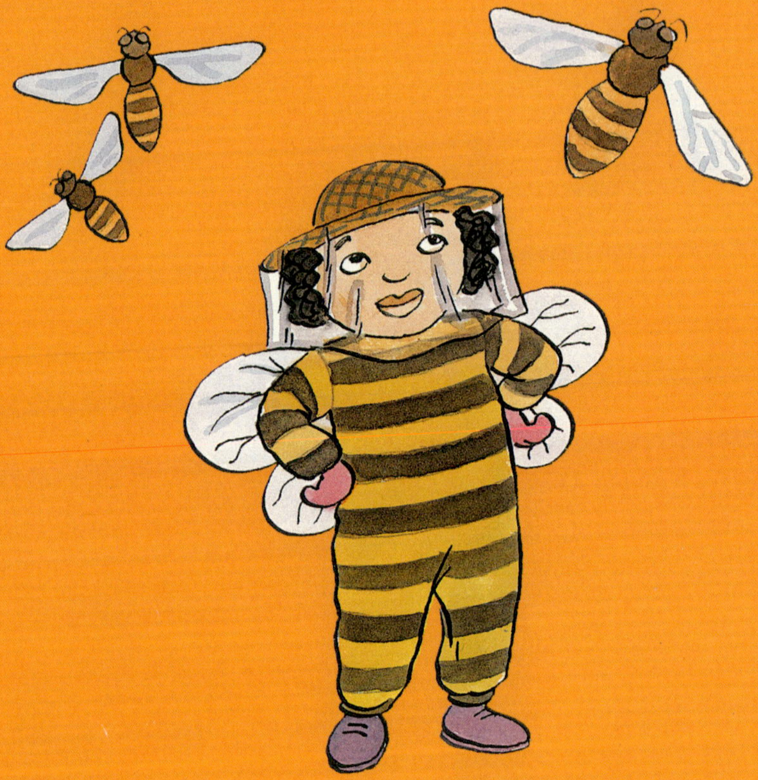

I like bees.

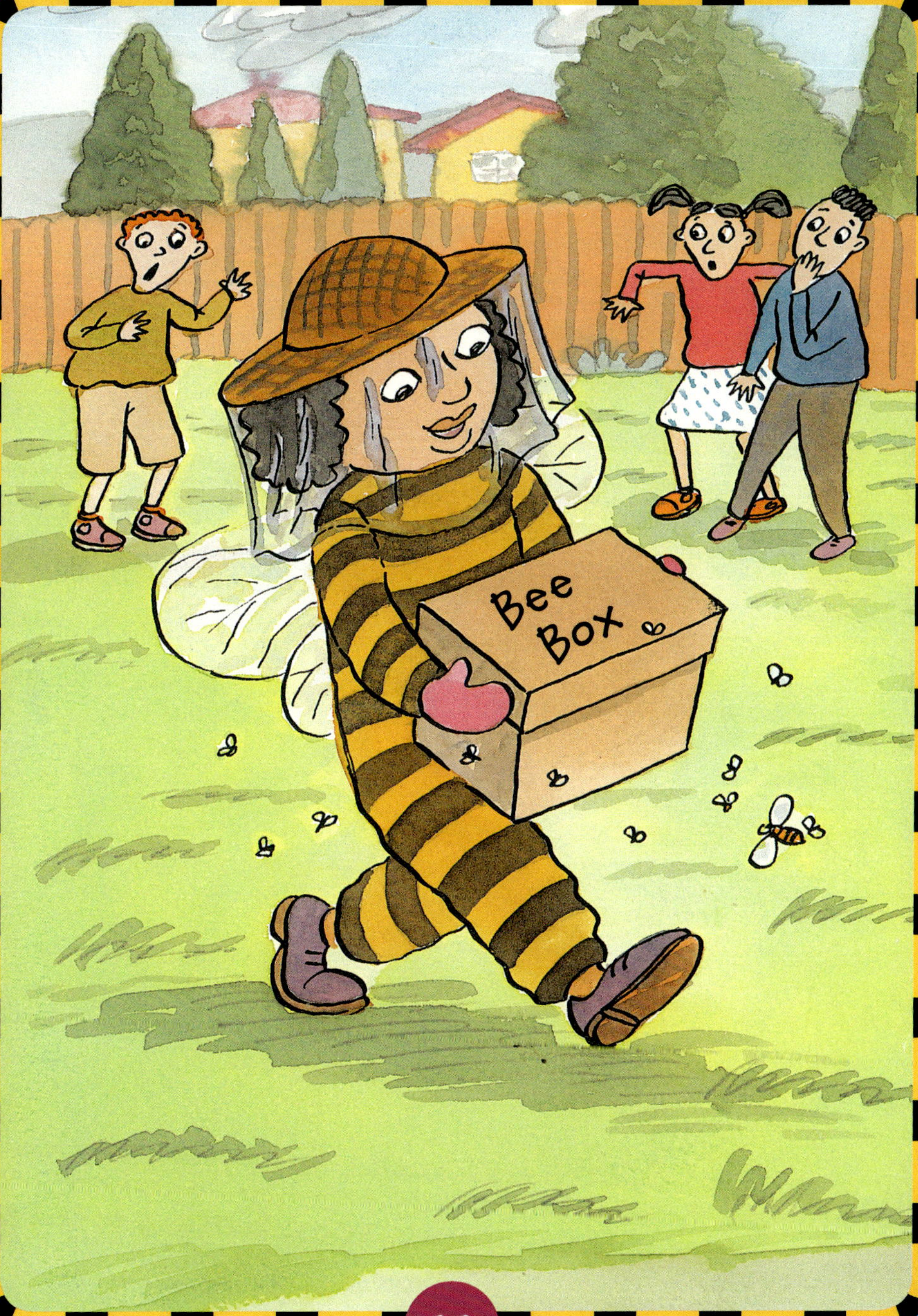
Bee Box

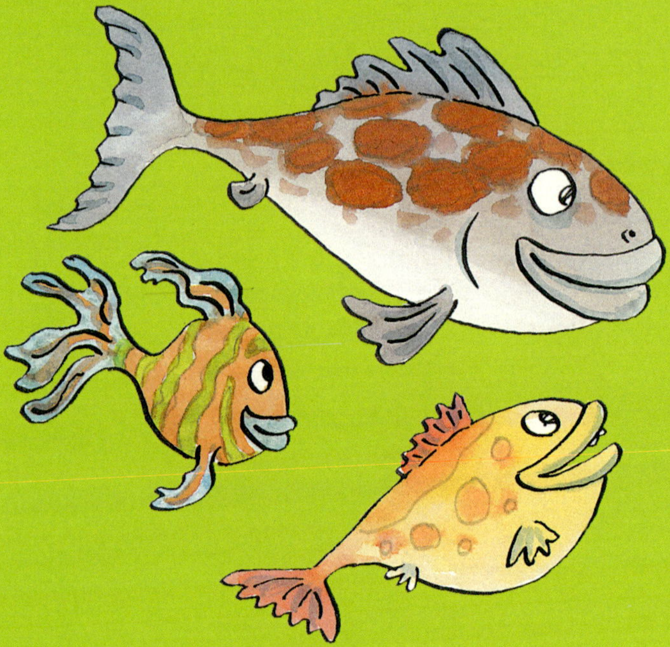

I like fish.

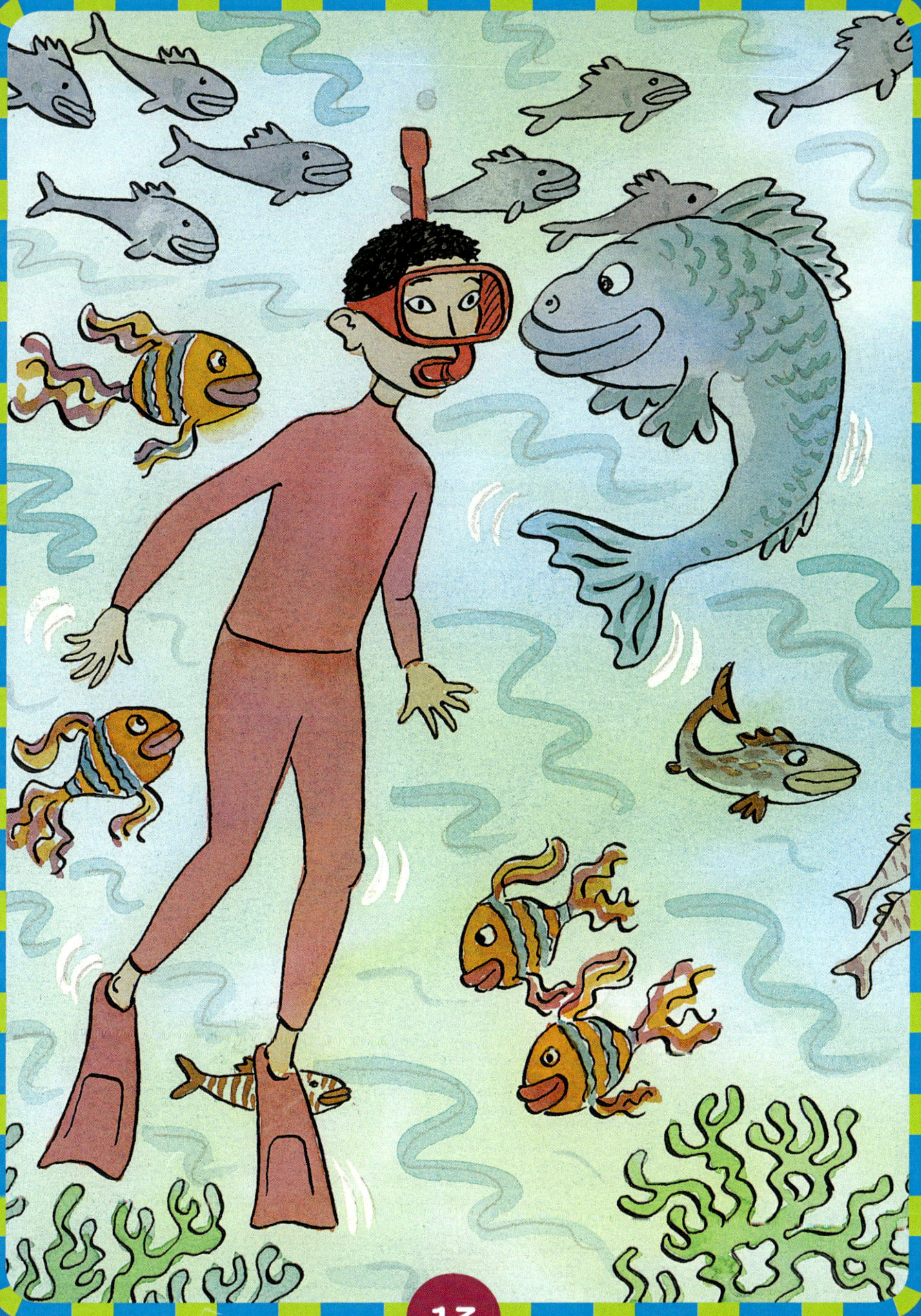

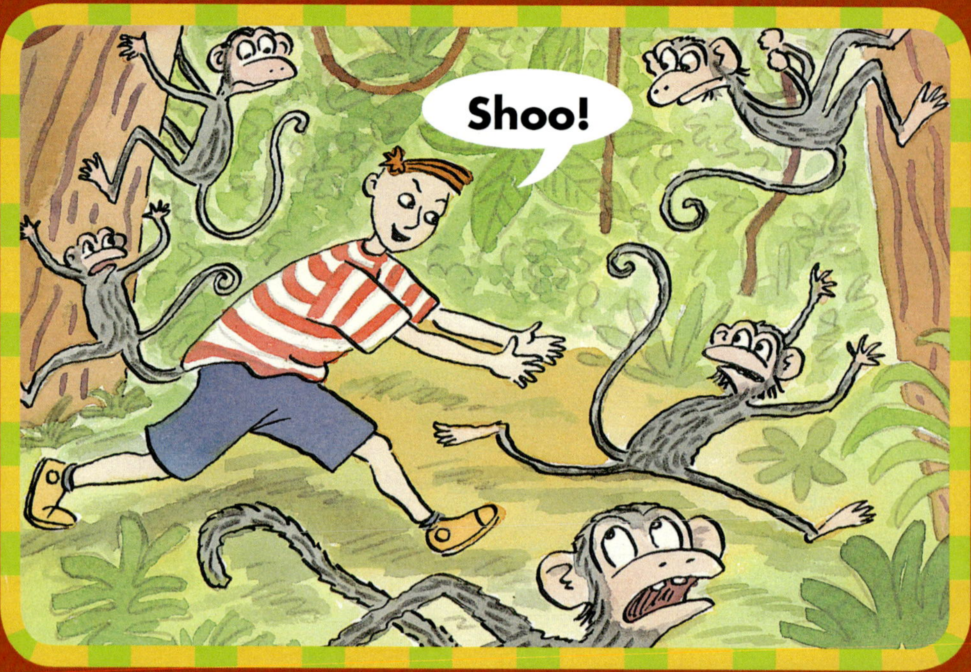
Shoo!

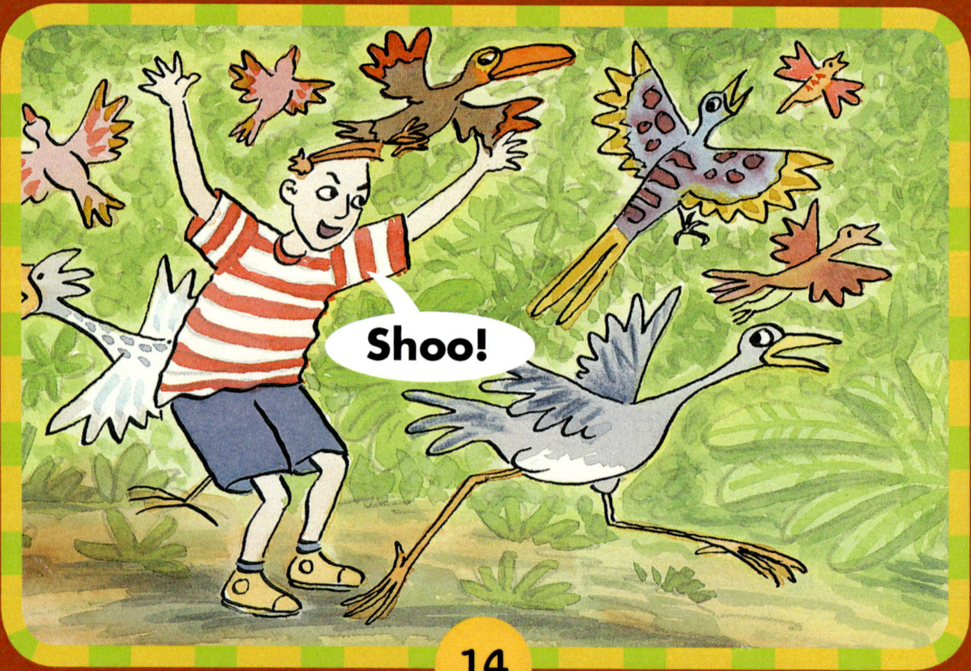
Shoo!

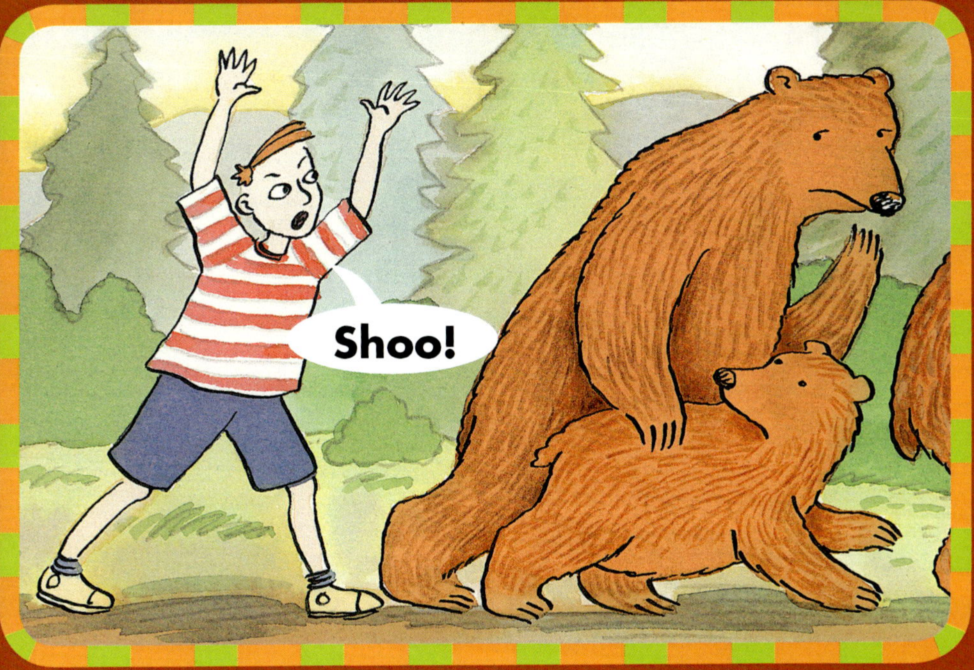
Shoo!

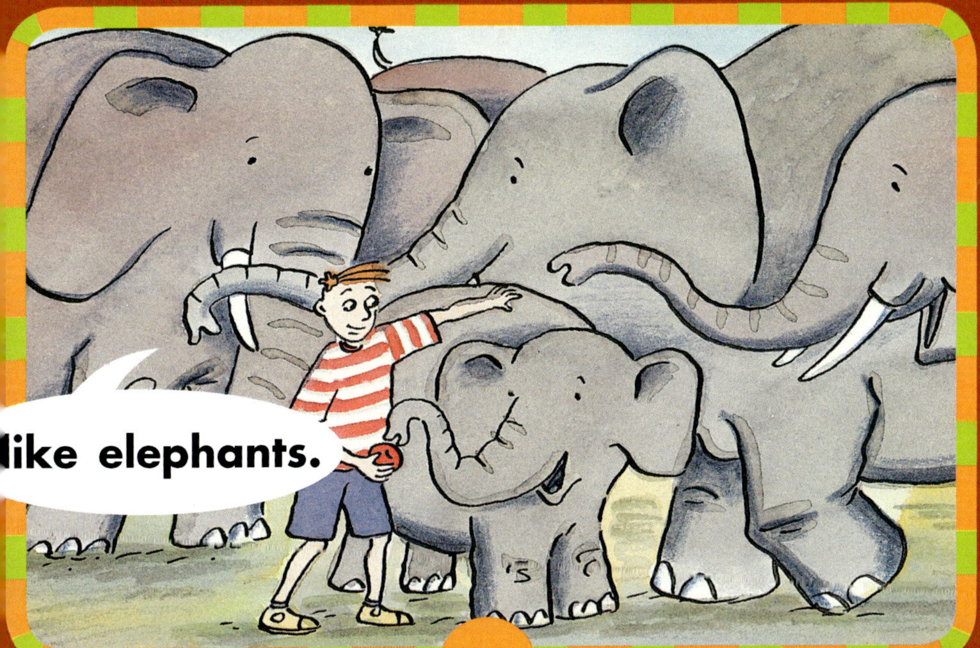
like elephants.

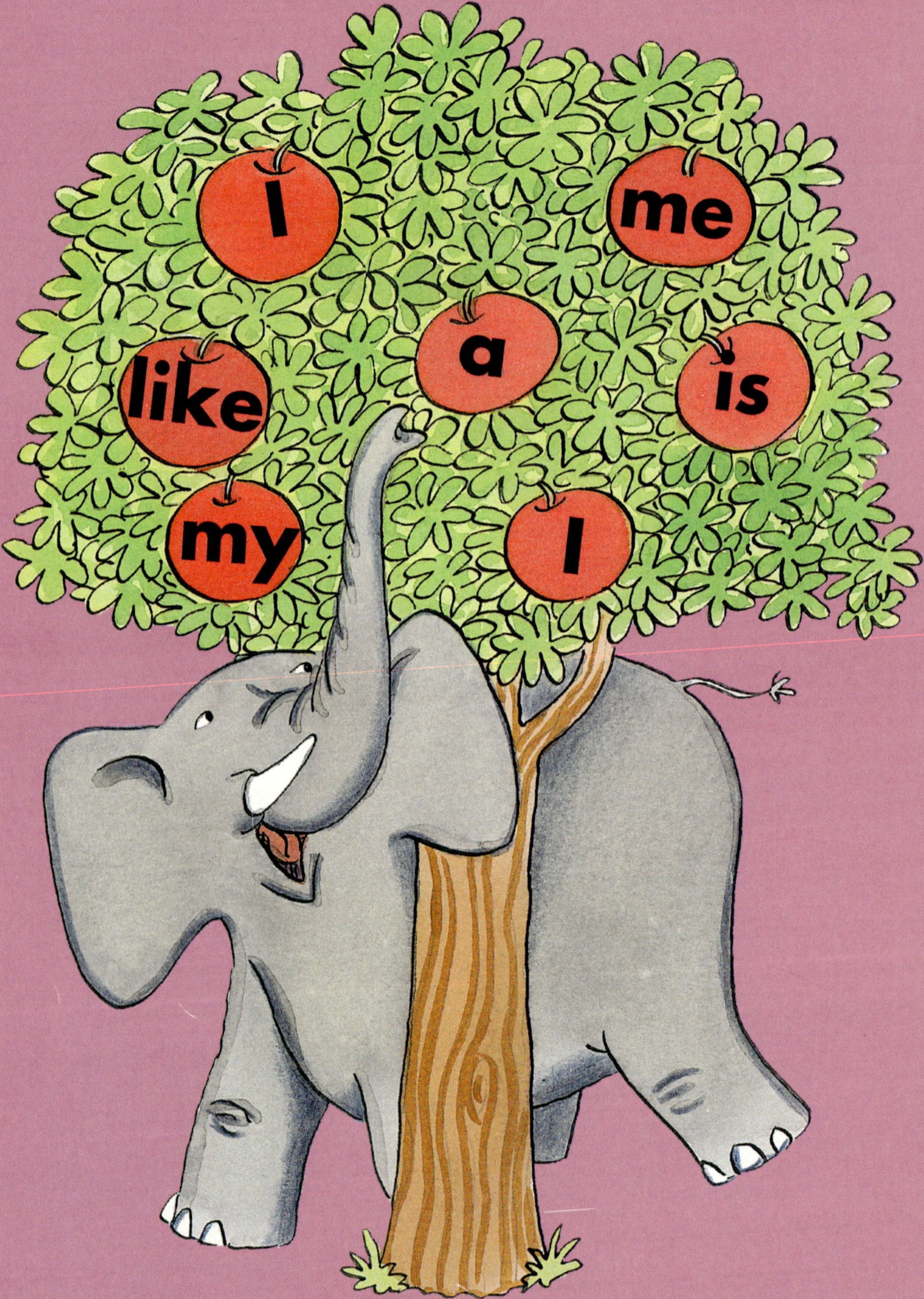
I
me
a
like
is
my
I